Dark Pine:
Tales of Terror

BY Christina DeHaan

Dark Pine: Tales of Terror

Cover Image: Christina DeHaan
Illustrations: Christina DeHaan
Layout: Christina DeHaan

Printed in the U.S.A.
ISBN: 979-8-3304-3764-1

Christina DeHaan
Middletown, NJ 07748

returntowriting@aol.com
https://sites.google.com/view/chrissy-tina-t

This book contains scenes of violence, gore, and strong language.

Dedicated to the curious souls who love urban legends and wished they were true

Dark Pine

Pine

Tales of Terror

Christina DeHaan

DARK PINE: TALES OF TERROR

Table of Contents:

Welcome to Dark Pine

Urban legends. Stories passed down from generation to generation. Where they began is often a mystery, but one thing's for certain, they continue to instill fear and curiosity. From the local haunted house at the end of the street, to creatures that lurk in the shadows. Every town has them. Every city and every state. Every piece of land holds a story, a legend. For the curious adventurer these legends are challenges. To teens they invite dares, something only the brave dig into. No matter who seeks them out the truth may be scarier than the tales that reeled them in.

The Door to Nowhere

To Mark and Sam it was just another weekend. The door wasn't too far from Sam's house. They'd heard the stories. They figured, why not check it out, it's only a door after all. What's the harm?

The building the door was a part of sat in an old, abandoned part of the Main Street area of Dark Pine. Tucked away through a dense forest of shrubs and overgrowth, it loomed over what was left of its old parking lot. The boys had heard of the door from classmates and parents throughout the years. Some said it was a portal to another dimension. Most agreed it was only a door, more than likely left over from a catwalk that was either taken down or lost to time. What everyone knew though, was that anyone who went looking for the door rarely made it back, and the few who did were never the same.

No one really knew what happened within the building itself. At one point it had been a warehouse. At another it was home to the homeless before the shelter was built. Yet somehow, somewhere along its timeline, the door became its only identifier. Before the new shelter was built further into town, there were reports of people going missing. At the time it was assumed that these people just went their own way, maybe they wandered off in the middle of the night. After the shelter opened though, that's when the legend started. Locals started daring each other to venture in. Attempts to stay the night became popular. It was the new hangout for the kids, until more people started to disappear.

It started with one or two kids here and there. Officers explained it away calling them runaways. While the parents didn't agree, they reluctantly gave in over time. Eventually, the first story of the door claiming a victim emerged one night after a group of high schoolers dared each other to stay the night. They were getting ready for the night in one of the second-floor rooms when one of their friends noticed the door along the wall. They called out to the group, joking about the drop when the others heard the door open and close. When they called out to their friend and there was no response they went to check. He was gone. Nowhere to be seen. They checked the whole building, calling out to him in hopes it was all a bad joke to no avail. He was gone and so were they. They booked it out of the building and rushed to the police who wrote them off as another group of local pranksters. When their friend never showed the next day for school and they'd all been called into the main office during second period, they knew what had happened.

Since then, it'd become a local legend, "The Door to Nowhere" is what they called it. The stories didn't stop more kids from taking the challenge to stay the night. They all wanted to know if it was true. Luckily, most were too afraid to approach the door, but that didn't keep more disappearances from happening. Like most kids before them Sam and Mark gave into their curiosity. It couldn't be true, right?

Pushing their way through the brush, Sam and Mark started their journey towards the building. Two kids that were told not to go near the building, and you know what happens when you tell someone not to do something.

"Are you sure about this?" Sam asked, shoving a branch out of his way, trying to keep up with Mark.

"We've gone over this, Sam. It's gonna be fine," Mark said, powering ahead. "Are you really gonna chicken out now? Come on!"

The two ducked and dodged low hanging branches, nearly tripping over sprawling roots and lumps of grass that grew through the old, cracked concrete.

Sam finally caught up to his friend. "I'm not chickening out," he insisted. "It's just...you know the stories."

Holding back some brush to see through to figure out the best path forward, Mark kept his eyes ahead as he responded. "Yeah, and you're dumb enough to believe 'em."

"Then what happened to everyone?" Sam nervously snapped back.

Mark turned back to his friend. "You know what happened. They left. There's no way anything actually happened to them." He turned back to the clearing he made. "We're almost there. Let's go."

With a sigh of defeat Sam followed after. Crouching through a small tunnel of branches, the two made their way to a clearing that opened up, revealing a rusted chain link fence. On the other side, towering over them, was the old building. Two stories up the door sat, its green paint chipped and flaking, nothing beneath it but a clear drop to the ground below. The two stood there in silence and awe.

Clearing his throat, Mark gave a nervous laugh to break the tension. "There it is," he said as the reality of the whole thing set in. "It's just a door. I'm gonna walk up there, open it, and you're just gonna walk away disappointed."

The two walked over to a hole in the fence that surrounded the old warehouse. Mark crouched down and crawled through, dirt and gravel crunching beneath his hands and feet as he made his way through.

"So, you really wanna go up there?" Sam asked, crawling his way through once Mark made it to the other side.

Mark looked up at the door in the warehouse wall, his confidence waning, but he refused to show it. "Yeah. It's just a door. There's nothing to worry about." Pulling out his phone he looked back at Sam. "Get ready."

He walked up the steps to the front door, it was barely hanging onto the hinges. A board covered in graffiti lay on the ground from previous brave souls that came here before them. Stepping into the threshold, Mark disappeared into the dark of the warehouse leaving Sam outside ready to see him open the door to nowhere.

Sam stood a good ten feet from the building with his eyes on the door above him. Phone out, he called Mark. "So, you ready?"

"Yup. It's right in front of me. Ready for me to prove you wrong?"

Sam sighed and chuckled, "Yeah, go ahead. Open the door and let's see who's wrong."

The ground was littered with old newspapers and garbage that had been worn and torn from the weather. On the side of the warehouse were some old missing persons flyers taped up and rippled from the rain. It was just a rumor. No one truly believed the door was a portal. But so many people had gone missing. Supposedly they all came here for the same reason, to open the door. No one had ever actually opened it. It was probably just locked. But what if it was true? What if it really was a portal?

"Alright, I'm about to turn the handle," Mark said over the phone. "Get ready for the photo op there, Sammy."

Sam stood there ready to see the door open.

Nothing.

Sam gave it a second, waiting for anything. This had to be a joke. "Mark, come on. Quit joking around and open the door."

"It is open. I'm looking right at you."

Nerves started getting the better of him. "Mark, quit it. Just open the door. This isn't funny."

"Sam, I mean it. It's open. You're looking right at me. If anyone's gotta quit joking around it's you."

The door was closed. No sign of Mark. Just the closed door. Dread covered Sam's face. He held the phone up to his ear and ran inside. "I'm coming in. Just stay where you are."

That's how it happened.

That's how it always happened.

They hear about the door, the missing people. They want to see it for themselves.

Sometimes a door is just a door. It just doesn't always lead to where you expect it to.

The Staircase

The tower was a historic landmark, the center of the old town before it uprooted, moving to a bigger clearing to become the Dark Pine of today. The old town had been left to time, untouched by humans and worn by the elements. Grass overgrown. Trees took over the few homes that still surrounded the tower. Other homes left abandoned. Roads, the few there were, now broken down.

Now the tower, or what's left of it, watched over a ghost town in every sense of the term. But it holds more than history. To the people in Dark Pine it's become another urban legend of sorts. Inside the tower a staircase spirals up the center. Unlike the walls that surround it, the stairs have remained seemingly untouched and intact. The building once stood as a watch tower and town hall when the town first formed. Now it sits as a reminder of what was and has become a popular haunt for the brave to venture.

The stairs, you see, were so perfectly preserved that people have become drawn to them. Peeking over the remaining walls the stairs almost seem to watch you. Over the years people have tried to climb them. Some reported hearing footsteps behind them when they were the only ones on them. Others reported hearing tapping on the railing. But some claim that it's haunted by the spirit of a woman who supposedly fell from the steps one day on a dare to spend the night on the steps. Legend has it an unseen force led her to the top of the staircase and pushed her off. Those brave enough to follow in her footsteps and spend the night claim to see her at the top of the steps, asking them to join her.

"And now you're following in *their* footsteps? Seriously, John? This is so dumb," Lucy said, leaning against the brick of the school wall waiting for him to finish gathering his things from his locker.

"No, *we're* following in their footsteps," he clarified. With a tinny metallic squeak the locker door shut as John slung his backpack over his shoulder. "I'm not going alone."

The two started off down the hall, joining the crowd of other students herding their way out of the building, ready to enjoy the weekend.

"Why do I have to go with you? I thought you were brave enough to go alone," Lucy mocked.

"Yeah, well, I wanna have someone to share the victory with of surviving the night," John responded, lightly elbowing her in the arm.

"Let me guess, Ricky turned you down," Lucy said, raising a brow.

After a brief moment of awkward silence, he gave a sigh of defeat. "Fine, you're right. He thought I was joking about staying overnight."

Fighting back laughter, Lucy put an arm around him, pulling him into a side hug and patting him on the chest. "Don't worry, I'll go with you," she confirmed. "I'll even try my best not to say I told you so when nothing happens."

"That's *really* reassuring," John said. "I mean, my ego's a little bruised, but I'll take it."

~

Later that night, at John's house, the two met up, prepping for the weekend ahead. Lucy sat on the bed as John packed his bag for the trip to the tower. The two were mostly silent as a random punk song played through static on the radio. Lucy bobbed her head to the beat, but John couldn't be bothered.

"Come on," she started. "You can't tell me you're taking this seriously. It's just some stairs and an old ghost story. There's nothing to worry about."

Shoving some more things into his bag he responded, "Yeah, but it's also still surrounded by forest. Do you wanna risk getting attacked by a bear?"

"A bear? We have a higher chance of getting chased by a deer than a bear out there," Lucy joked.

"Joke all you want, but you won't be laughing when you have to run up those stairs from a bear or a wolf," John insisted.

Lucy choked on a laugh. "So there are wolves out there now? Forget the ghosts, are you sure you're ready for the wildlife?"

"*Ha ha*, very funny," he sassed back. "You can't blame me for playing it safe. Fumbling through the bag one more time, he zipped it shut. "So, you ready Luce?"

Hopping off the bed, Lucy walked over to the bedroom door. "As ready as I'll ever be," she said.

"Hold on, where's your stuff?" John asked.

Lucy reached down to grab her bag that had been leaning against the doorframe the whole time. "Right here."

"Did you even actually pack for this or is that just your homework?"

"Yeah. I grabbed a few snacks, a blanket, and I have my jacket. Other than that, my cellphone, wallet, and everything else are in here," she said picking up the purse that was hidden under the backpack.

"And I thought I was overpacking," John joked. "Why didn't you put that stuff in the backpack?"

"What? The blanket and jacket took up most of the space. That and I did actually bring my homework too," she answered.

John shot her a look.

"What? I doubt there's gonna be a lot to do there. It's an old staircase in a rotting building," she said. Raising her purse and adjusting it over her shoulder, she continued. "Plus, you have pockets for extra storage. I don't. A purse is a girl's best friend. We can live out of these things. I may not have much in the backpack, but I've got plenty in here." She proudly pat the side of her bag.

"Alright, let's get going then," John said.

On their way down the stairs, a voice called out from the living room. "You two heading out?" John's dad asked as the two paused by the front door. "It's getting dark out there."

"Heading over to Lucy's place," John said.

Lucy whacked him in the arm. "You didn't tell them?"

"Didn't tell us what?" Joining them in the foyer, his dad stood at the entrance way to the living room, hands on his hips.

"It's nothing," John said.

14

He crossed his arms. "Nothing, huh?" John's father looked from John to Lucy and back to John. "Where are you two actually going?"

"Well... You see..." John scratched his head, struggling to get a word out.

"We're going camping. He didn't want you to worry. It's just for the night," Lucy intercepted.

"Nice save," John said under his breath to her.

"Camping? Where *exactly* are you gonna be camping?" His father asked.

"The woods at the edge of town," Lucy started. "By the old tower."

"So much for the save," John said, nudging Lucy.

"Let me guess, you're going to the stairs," his father said with a judging look, crossing his arms.

The two nodded in unison.

Hanging his head in, what John assumed was more than likely disappointment, his dad let out a long sigh. "You've heard the stories?"

They nodded.

"You know what I think about the stories. They're just that, stories." His father paused, watching John and Lucy hanging on his words. "It's just for tonight?"

The two nodded again.

"Well," he started. "I'll let you go. Back when I was your age I would've done the same thing if I heard about something like that."

John and Lucy's faces lit up in a combination of disbelief and joy at his father's response. "Really?" John asked.

"Mmhmm." His dad nodded. "Just be careful. And don't forget to call when you're on your way back. Your mother would kill me if anything happened to you."

"Thanks dad!" John said, running over to hug him. "I promise we'll be back before you know it." With his father's approval, the two were off to the tower to spend the night at the staircase.

~

John's car stuttered as he turned the key. It wasn't the newest ride, but it was better than nothing. It worked for his brother, so it was good enough for him to take on when his brother upgraded to a new model. After a few tries the engine roared to life. Patting the steering wheel with pride, John put the car in reverse and began to pull it out.

"If this is how the night's starting, I think we're gonna be camping in the car wherever it breaks down instead," Lucy joked.

"Hey, if it can get me to school and back. It should be able to handle a little road trip," John said.

Lucy looked out the window, taking in the view of the neighborhood. Each house similar to the next, the only real differences being the colors of the siding and the front yards. Not much variety, but it was a cozy place to call home. House after house they made their way through the belly of town. The old town was just on the other side of Dark Pine. While it wasn't too big, it was still a significant drive for John's old car. It'd definitely seen better days. Just barely on it's frame, nowadays it sounded like a racecar, though the neighbors didn't seem to mind.

Lucy flinched every now and then noticing the old cigarette burns on the roof from when the car belonged to John's brother. "You really need to get that fixed. That's the tenth time now in this thing."

"It's not my fault you keep forgetting they're there," John said, smirking.

"Yeah, well I wouldn't be freaking out thinking there were spiders in the car if you just took this thing in to get fixed," she jabbed back.

"Hey, maybe there's a few actual spiders hiding in here. You never know. I did recently clean off some webbing on your side the other day," he said.

"Not funny, John," Lucy responded, looking around her and scratching her arm. "Please tell me you're joking. You know I hate spiders."

"I'm kidding," he started. "The webs were under the back seat."

Lucy whacked him in the arm. "We're taking this in when we get back, you hear me?"

Fighting back a chuckle, John answered, "Sure thing. You're helping me pay though since you suggested it. You know I can't afford it."

"That's fine. If it means I don't have to deal with those burn marks on the roof, I'll happily chip in," she responded.

Making their way down Main Street, they passed the local hot spots. The street was hopping as it usually was on a Friday, even for as late as it was. Crowds lined up outside the cinema for the last showings of the night.

"We could just pull over and see a movie instead. You know I've been wanting to see *There Can Only Be One* for a while now," Lucy said. "We can always check out the stairs another night."

"We can *also* see the movie another night." John quickly looked over at Lucy who was slumping back in the passenger seat. "Look, I know this isn't what you wanted to do. We can see the movie tomorrow night if you want. Would that make up for this?"

Readjusting how she was sitting, she turned to him. "Promise?"

"I promise," John said. "Let's just get through the night first."

With a few more stutters and sputters of the car at a couple of lights, the two finally reached the edge of the old town. The entrance to the town was more than a little overgrown. Trees had reached over either side creating a tunnel of sorts. Branches hung down over the roof and hood of the car, sweeping over it as it rocked over bumps as it passed under. Through the trees the town opened up into a field of tall grass and weeds. Old decaying homes circled the edge of the town. Driving further into the area the remains of the old tower loomed ahead of them, the top of the stairs peaking over the walls, watching them as they parked the car.

The town itself was quiet as the two stepped out of the car. Only the whistle of the wind through the surrounding trees and the occasional caw of a crow could be heard. Not a soul in sight. Graffiti on the sides of the houses and the remaining walls of the tower greeted them as they gathered their things from the trunk.

"This place gives me the creeps," Lucy said, slinging her backpack over her shoulders.

"Yeah," John agreed. "The stories don't prep you for seeing the real thing. Look at this stuff." He walked over to the outer wall of the tower where some words of warning had been sprayed onto the brick. "She'll take you down with her? Sounds like it's gonna be a fun night then."

"Get your mind out of the gutter," Lucy said lightly shoving him as she walked by with her bags.

"What?" He laughed. "You're the one with your mind in the gutter. I was just thinking of how she's probably gonna pull one of us to the top of the stairs and drag us with her on the fall."

"Let's just get everything set up," Lucy insisted. "The sooner we get this over with the better."

The entrance to the tower was still pretty much intact. Granted, the door itself was more of a doormat than an actual door at this point, but Lucy and John stepped over it and into the belly of the beast. Inside the tower the stone walls held the remains of rotted wooden shelves. Rusted sconces barely hung onto their spots in the walls. On the few tables that still stood were old papers and books, mostly deteriorated from weather and time. Along the higher half of the walls broken beams held up whatever remained of the upper floors. In the center of the space the staircase stood strong. Just as the stories told, it was in the best condition compared to the rest of the tower. At the base of the steps empty water bottles and food wrappers lay scattered from previous adventurers daring to spend the night. Beneath the rubbish and rubble red spray paint could be seen peaking through.

John walked over to the steps to get a closer look. "Wonder what's under there." Kneeling down, he reached out, about to move the trash.

"John, don't touch that! You don't know where that's been!" Lucy rushed in, pulling him back a bit before he could touch any of the garbage.

"It's an old water bottle. The only place it's been is here," John said.

"At least like kick it out of the way. I'm not risking you getting sick because of something you touched," Lucy said.

Pushing himself back up on his feet, John used his foot to sweep some of the trash out of the way revealing a creepy looking symbol. "Woah."

"Are you sure we should really spend the night here?"

"Yeah, it's gonna be great." John turned to Lucy, he could see the concern in her eyes. "Don't worry. That's probably old anyway. No one really comes out here much anymore. Besides..." He slid the backpack off of his shoulder and reached in. "I've got more than enough in here to keep us safe," he said, pulling out a hefty flashlight and tossing it up making it flip before catching it. "We'll be just fine."

The night grew darker as they laid out blankets by the base of the stairs. John dug through his bag and pulled out a few small battery lanterns. Placing them around the area, he handed one to Lucy, giving her a comforting smile to ease the nerves. Deeper and deeper into the bag he dug, pulling more tools out and setting up a basecamp of sorts around the steps. On the bottom few steps, he placed a few smaller flashlights. It wasn't until he pulled out a thing of salt to line the steps that Lucy intercepted.

"What are you doing?" she asked.

"Setting things up. I've almost got it all ready," he answered, making sure the flashlights were just loose enough that even the slightest touch could turn them on.

Rubbing her face, Lucy put a hand on her hip and walked over to John. "I mean, *this*. What is all *this* for? I thought we were just camping out here for a stupid dare or something."

"It's to see if the stories are real," he said.

"What?"

"The flashlights are to communicate with the girl that fell and the salt will show us if anyone's walked in it," John explained.

"I'm starting to see why Ricky turned you down," Lucy commented.

"Come on, it's gotta seem a little cool to you, right? You're the one that likes all of the horror movies. This is right up your alley." John crossed his arms and looked at her with a brow raised.

"Yeah, but horror movies are just that, movies. I know the difference between fantasy and reality,

John. Besides, even if I did believe this stuff, isn't salt supposed to ward things off?" She gestured to the layer of salt that covered three steps.

Scratching his head he looked back at the stairs and frowned. "Shit. You're right." He turned back to Lucy. "Maybe she's a good spirit and it won't affect her." He shrugged giving a weak smile.

"Well, I'm gonna get some homework done. You do whatever it is you came here to do," she said, making her way back to her bags, trying not to trip on everything along the way.

"You just wait and see," John started. "This is gonna be epic."

~

Hours passed with nothing to show. Lucy had bunched up her backpack as a makeshift pillow and used her jacket like a blanket. John sat on the bottom step, flipping the flashlight in his hands. The air grew colder as the wind picked up. Checking his watch, John looked over his shoulder up the stairs. Both flashlights he'd placed remained off and the salt he'd lined the steps in was unbothered. With a sigh of defeat he stood up from the step.

"I'm starting to think you were right," John said, walking over to Lucy and sitting down next to her.

With a grumble, she rolled over to face him. "Mmhmm," she mumbled. "It's just a story."

"I guess it was all for nothing."

"Hey, at least now you know," Lucy said, reaching out and patting him on the arm. "Now let's call it a night and get some sleep."

Reluctantly he agreed and grabbed his own bag and propped it up as his pillow, then wrapped himself in the exposed part of the blanket he'd laid out beneath him. Before he knew it he was out like a light. By the time a rattle woke him up so were the other lights, out. Not a single one was on even though he was sure he'd put new batteries in them before they left. As his eyes adjusted to the darkness, a beam of light sprung to life behind him.

Nudging Lucy he tried his best to wake her. "Lucy," he whispered. "Luce. Wake up. You've gotta see this."

Unfortunately, she just groaned and shrugged it off.

"Come on. The flashlight turned on by itself!" He excitedly whispered, trying again to nudge her awake.

Lucy swung her arm at him, groaning again.

From somewhere in the darkness beyond the flashlight another rattle echoed in the night.

"Where is that coming from?" John asked.

The rattle rang out again, sounding distant yet somehow closer.

Squinting, John raised a hand to his eyes, hoping maybe it would make it easier to see anything beyond the light. "Is anyone there?!" A loud groan caught his attention.

From the ground beside him, Lucy gave another groan and frustratedly pushed herself up into a sitting position. "Yeah, I'm here," she moaned, her voice a gravelly half-asleep rasp. "What's going on?"

"The lanterns all went out and the flashlight on the step turned on by itself and there's this weird rattle I keep hearing. I think it's somewhere on the stairs, but I can't see anything." The words just flooded out of his mouth.

"Just grab the flashlight and shine it up the stairs," Lucy said, rubbing her eyes and giving into a long yawn. "What happened to the flashlight from earlier?"

"Right, the flashlight." John threw back the blanket and fumbled around, feeling for it in the darkness. Sliding his hand under his bag, his fingers wrapped around the flashlight he'd been playing with earlier. "Got it!" He flicked it on, briefly blinding himself, then turned around and aimed it up the steps.

Nothing. Not a single animal or pebble in sight, just step after step all the way up the spiral.

"Weird." He reached over to the flashlight on the step, but before he could reach it it turned off. "Huh?"

"Did that just?" Lucy rubbed her eyes again, blinking repeatedly trying to make sense of what just happened. "You touched that, right? If not then there must've been a breeze or something. Right?" Every ounce of sleep that had been trying to tell her to close her eyes was gone.

"No. My hand wasn't even on it," John insisted.

The rattle returned, followed by a few small pebbles tumbling down the steps, landing at the edge of their blankets. The two sprung to their feet, staying close to each other.

"What was that?" Lucy asked, gripping onto John's arm.

"That's what I was trying to tell you about," he explained.

"I think we should go," Lucy said.

The rattling grew louder as more pebbles rolled down the steps. A faint tapping started up causing the layer of dust and grime on the railing to shake and kick up.

"Did you hear that?" John asked.

Lucy nodded, shaking as fear began to settle in. "I really think we should go now, John." Lightly tugging him away from the stairs.

John raised his flashlight, trying his best to shine it up the spiral, hoping it would reveal anything that could possibly be making the noise. Like before, there was nothing. "Hello?! Is anyone there?"

Lucy tugged at his arm harder this time. "What are you doing? Let's get out of here."

"Hold on, I just want to be sure it's not like an animal or something," John insisted, stepping forward and wriggling free from Lucy's grip.

"Are you crazy? Whatever it is it's freaking me out. Let's go!" She tried to reach out to him, but he already started up the steps.

One step at a time John slowly walked up the stairs. One hand firmly on the railing and the other gripping onto his flashlight for dear life. The salt he'd laid out crunched under his feet as he kept going. As he continued further up the stairs the rattle and tapping kept up. With each tap on the railing, he could feel it vibrating under his grip.

At the base of the stairs Lucy stood watching him, fear keeping her from following after him. She looked around the tower out into the darkness beyond the flashlight on the steps, eyes darting to every shadow she could just barely make out. Fight or flight was kicking in and she wasn't sure which to listen to. Looking back up the steps she could hear John's footsteps on the wooden steps. "John, do you see anything?!"

About halfway up the spiral, John could still hear the rattle and tapping. Somehow it still sounded close, yet with each step up it got further away. "Nothing yet!" He called back to Lucy. "It's like the sound's moving."

"It's probably nothing and we're both just freaking out over the wind or something. Come back down!" Lucy leaned into the railing, trying to look up through the spiral of the staircase. She could just see the light of John's flashlight making its way up the stairs and the vague shape of him past the light. Squinting into the darkness around John, Lucy could just make out another shape behind him, a black blob following close. "John!" She grabbed one of the flashlights from the steps and started up the steps in a panic.

"I think I'm getting closer!" John called back, still following the rattle and tap like a sailor to a siren call.

"John, behind you!" Lucy screamed to him, flashlight in hand, its light dancing from step to step as she tried to bolt up after the the black mass that trailed close behind John.

Nearing the top of the staircase, John couldn't see anything on the last few steps that could possibly be making the noise.

"John!" Lucy tried again to get his attention.

Turning around toward the railing, John flashed his light back down the stairs. "Yeah

Luce?" The beam of light met a shadowy mass. Just beyond it he could see Lucy frantically climbing the steps. Looking into the darkness of the blob a face began to form. It was faint at first. Piercing blue eyes emerging from the void, then the mouth and nose.

In a soft calming tone, a woman's voice spoke. "Do you want to join me?"

Stumbling back he fell on the steps, reaching out to the railing and gripping onto it as tightly as he could with both hands. His flashlight rolled off the steps and down the middle of the spiral. From the darkness a hand reached out. Those blue eyes seemed to glow in the dark of the night, watching him as he tried to look away. Closer and closer the hand got. A cold tingle starting on his chin and sweeping under as the hand slid over his face, gently pulling his gaze back till their eyes met again.

"Don't be afraid," the entity said. "It will feel like flying."

"Let him go!" A beam of light burst through the darkness and through the middle of the mass as Lucy aimed her flashlight at it.

The void swirled as the face and hand dissipated. The flashlight beam grew bigger as the mass disappeared.

Rushing up to John, Lucy reached out her hand to pull him back on his feet. "You alright?"

"I think so," John shakily answered. "Let's get out of here."

The two hurried down the stairs and back to their things. Shoving what they could back into their bags, they legged it back to the car, blankets sticking out and dragging on the ground behind them. Throwing open the driver and passenger side doors they hopped in and tossed their bags in the back. John fumbled through his pockets for the keys, almost dropping them as he pulled them out. The car stuttered and rumbled with each turn of the key in the ignition.

"Come on. Come on," he grumbled with each turn. "You can do this. Don't break down on me now."

"Hurry! Hurry!" Lucy yelled.

"I'm trying!" He snapped, still trying to force each turn of the key.

Lucy looked out the window back up at the tower, the top of the stairs peaking over the wall. Her heart sank as she could see against the night sky the faint form of a figure at the top of the stairs, two faint blue dots watching them. "Holy shi— Go! Go! Go!"

As if by some miracle the car sprang to life. "Yes!" John cheered.

Off into the night they drove. Back to the safety of Dark Pine. Back to the safety of Lucy's home. Anywhere but near the tower.

Whitmoore Manor

The house stood empty for well over a decade on the corner of Redline and Warren. Families had come and gone, but none stayed more than a few months to a year. Each came in with hopes of a new start, settling down in the humble town of Dark Pine, but it never panned out. Each left with their own share of stories. Moving objects, bumps in the night, all the tell-tale signs of a haunted house. There was one problem with those stories though, those weren't the reasons the families moved out.

The house in question was known as Whitmoore Manor. Back in the 1800's Robert Whitmoore and his wife Emily moved into the house with their two children Charlie and Lily. They'd moved in when Robert had inherited a local plant from his father. All was going well at first. They seemed like any happy family. It wasn't until an unhappy feud between Robert and his close friend, Wilson Wright, he'd brought into the business that things took a turn.

Wilson was like a brother to him, a family friend. When Robert took the plant, however, Wilson had other plans. Some say he was driven to insanity. Others claim he'd had enough. Some even think he was overcome with jealousy over Robert taking the plant when Wilson had worked there for years and was supposedly close to a promotion. Whatever the reason was, one night before the end of his shift, Wilson barged into Robert's office and went off on him. The other workers thought it was just another dispute, a simple argument. It wasn't out of the ordinary for the two since Robert took over. When Wilson stormed after Robert though, following him out of the plant, no one thought he'd go as far as he would.

Blinded by rage, Wilson followed Robert all the way back to the house. It wasn't until Robert reached the front steps that Wilson threw the first punch. Neighbors reported hearing the screams as Emily opened the door and saw the two mid brawl, begging them to stop. One report recalls Robert calling back to her to get back in the house and lock the door. Despite the horror on Emily's face, Wilson continued his attack. Swing after swing, he refused to ease up.

It's believed that Emily ran back in the house and grabbed Robert's gun he kept in a drawer in the side table by his chair in the family room. She rushed back out the front and aimed in Wilson's direction, hoping that it would end the fight. She missed, hitting the tin mailbox instead. The shot was enough to distract Wilson and send him on a direct path to her. In a panic she reloaded the gun as she rushed inside, the only thing to give her time to slam the door behind her being Robert grabbing Wilson by the ankle to trip him as he lunged after her.

Robert was so beaten he could barely even crawl, but neighbors that came running after hearing the gunshot recount him pulling himself up the front steps, tears streaming down his face. From inside the house gunshots sounded off. By the time officers arrived it was too late. Wilson had done his worst and the damage was done. Robert watched as officers dragged Wilson out of the house kicking and screaming.

"So, why did the families move out?" Alex asked as the three of them stood outside Whitmoore Manor.

"Seriously, kid? What part of the story didn't you get?" Max responded. He turned to his other friend in frustration. "Brad, help me out here. You brought him along."

Brad huffed and sighed and walked over to Alex. "Look, people say they hear the screams of the family from that night."

"What?" Alex seemed more confused than curious. "How?"

Max shot Brad a look of disbelief.

"The family is said to haunt the house. Some said they've seen the children running in the halls and even seen Emily standing at the front door," Brad explained.

"Oh…What about Robert?" Alex asked, putting the pieces together.

Max and Brad exchanged looks.

"You wanna tell him?" Max asked.

"Fine," Brad said. "Robert was so overcome with regret for not being able to save his family he…" Brad stopped and looked back at Max. "Do you really want me to tell him that?"

"What? The story's already dark. Wilson killed the guy's family," Max said.

With a sigh of defeat, Brad looked back to Alex. "Let's just say that Robert didn't want to go on with the guilt he felt."

"So, they all haunt the place?" Alex looked up at the house.

As the trio stood there, another boy approached the group. "Hey guys, we goin' in or what?"

"Sup, Mike," Max said. "Yeah. We were just telling Alex here the story." He leaned in towards Mike, holding a hand up, blocking his mouth from Brad and Alex. "The kid's gonna be the end of us at the rate he asks questions."

"I'm sure he's not that bad," Mike insisted. He walked over to Brad and Alex. "How's it goin', I'm Mike."

"I'm Alex." Alex was happy to meet him. "You're Molly's brother, right?"

"Yeah," Mike said. "That's me." He looked back at Max who was fighting back a laugh. He returned his attention to Alex, "You ever been to Whitmoore Manor?"

"Nope. This is my first time. Brad said I could come along," Alex explained.

"He's just a kid, go easy on him," Brad said. "Mom said he had to come with us."

"Alright, alright." Mike put an arm around Alex. "I promise you, Alex, nothing's gonna happen. It's all just ghost stories to scare kids like you." He winked at Brad.

Brad face palmed and sighed as Max cracked a laugh at his expense.

"Let's just get this over with," Brad said.

"After you," Max said, gesturing towards the house.

Up the path the four walked, the house looming over them. It wasn't too big, but for a two-story home, in the fading light of the evening its windows looked like orange-red eyes staring down at them. Brad and Alex took the lead as Mike and Max hung back. Their whispers nearly blended with the evening breeze, but Brad could hear it all too well. He knew he shouldn't have brought Alex, but when their mom said he couldn't leave him home alone while her and their dad were out, Mike and Max were a little too eager to let him join the trip.

Despite the story and Brad's worries, Alex seemed content as they walked up the front steps. The area itself was mostly empty homes. The house sat just at the edge of town, so it was mostly abandoned for places closer to the main hub. The steps creaked under their feet. A light tapping could be heard as the wind swung a few branches against the upper windows. Alex wasn't too bothered by it, but Brad was more concerned with his friends than anything.

Behind the brothers the whispers continued. A few light chuckles snuck their way into the murmurs. Whatever they were saying, Brad wasn't having it. He spun around as the others caught up at the door. "Okay, get it out of your systems," he demanded.

Mike and Max looked at him, amused. "What?" Max asked, fighting back his remaining laughter. "It's nothing." He looked over Brad's shoulder at Alex, who was doing what he could to try and see through the dust and grime covered window in the door. "You wanna open it, for us, Alex?"

Alex looked back at them, surprised he'd been given the option. "Isn't it locked or something? I mean, it's been abandoned for years, right?"

"The cops gave up keeping an eye on this place years ago. No one's been around here in ages. Go for it," Max said.

Alex looked to his brother for approval.

While Brad didn't trust his friends, he nodded anyway. He was there and that's all that mattered. He just had to keep Alex close.

With Brad's approval Alex reached for the knob. It crackled in his grip as he gave it a turn. The door gave a similar crackle and creak as he pushed it open. A cool breeze picked up, sending a small collection of leaves that had piled on the top step into the house. "Woah." Slowly but carefully, he made his way in, Brad close behind him. "Look at this place." His eyes grew wide in wonder.

Despite the years and unwelcome guests that had left their marks in graffiti, it was nearly untouched to time. The furniture, though covered in blankets of dust and webbing, remained mostly intact. The center stairway greeted them with a railing of twisting designs etched into its molding that led up to the darkness of the second floor. The two stepped in further. It was hard to believe how much was still there.

"Hey guys, you've gotta see this," Brad said, calling back to Mike and Max. As soon as he'd said that the door slammed shut behind them. "Mike! Max!" Quick panic turned to frustration as he ran for the door, pulling on it in an attempt to force it open. "Come on guys, this isn't funny!"

Alex stood at the base of the stairs watching.

Still struggling with the door, he looked over his shoulder at his brother. "Are you gonna help me or what?"

As if pulled out of a trance, he rushed over to Brad's side and pulled the end of his sleeve over his hand. Wiping away the grime on glass, the two could just barely make out two figures walking away.

"Seriously?" Brad was done. He continued to struggle, jiggling the doorknob to no avail. "How the hell did they lock this thing?"

"I don't know," Alex said, watching the two warped figures of Mike and Max high five as they continued to the sidewalk. He turned back to the stairs, "You think we'll be stuck here?" he asked, his voice starting to shake a bit as nerves began to set in.

Catching the shift in his brother's voice, he put an arm around him, in reassurance. "We're gonna get out of here, I promise." He looked around, scanning the rooms off the sides. Aside from the little light that seeped in from the windows, it was mostly a dark haze of dust. "There's gotta be a back door. Let's try this way." Grabbing Alex by the hand, he pulled him along into the room to the left.

In the dim light of the setting sun that crept in, the haze of particles was clearer than ever. As they navigated their way through the room, it became clear they were headed the right way. Passing a couch against the wall and a coffee table decorated in web lined books and vases, they kept close making sure not to touch anything. Further back a faint gleam of sunlight guided them to a small nook next to what looked like a bathroom. Across form it was the entrance to the kitchen. From there Brad could see the back door.

"Yes!" He rushed over to the door and turned the knob. Going to pull it open, the knob came clean off leaving the door still closed. He held it up and turned to face his brother.

Baffled by the sight, Alex was speechless.

"So...it may not be what we hoped, but we can still figure something out," Brad assured him.

"What now?" Alex asked. The house groaned. "We can't stay here, Brad."

"I know, I know." Brad looked around, the doorknob still in hand. "Um..." His eyes landed on the window over the sink. "Do you think you can fit through that window?"

"What?" Alex looked at his brother, hoping he misheard him.

"That window. If I can get it open, do you think you could fit through?" Brad gestured to the window over the sink as he asked his brother again.

"I'm not climbing through that thing," Alex insisted.

"Look," Brad started. "Do you want out of here or not?"

"Well…" Alex looked at the window, unsure of how to answer. "I guess."

As Brad prepped to reach over the sink, a loud crash and thud shook the house, startling the boys.

"What the fuck was that?" Alex yelled, as he jumped.

"Language!" Brad whacked him in the arm.

"Seriously?! You heard that too, right?"

"Yeah, but that doesn't you can say that," Brad berated.

"What do you think it was?" Alex asked, looking back where they came from.

Brad didn't know what to say, but he tried his best to hide it. "The wind…yeah. That's it. It was probably the wind."

"The wind?" Alex was in disbelief. "That sounded like it was *in* the house, Brad. You don't think someone else is here, do you?"

"That's ridiculous, who else would..." He chucked the doorknob and rushed past his brother.

"Brad? Where are you going? Are you crazy? What if it's some psycho killer or something? Brad?!" No matter how hard he tried, Alex couldn't get his brother's attention.

Marching back to the foyer, a newfound rage building, Brad paused at the stairs. "Mike, Max, I know it's you! Where are you? This isn't funny?"

Catching his breath, Alex grabbed onto Brad by the shoulder, pulling him back. "What the hell are you doing?"

"It has to be them," Brad said through his teeth as another crash was heard from the second floor. Without hesitation he shrugged his brother off and stomped up the stairs.

Following after, Alex hurried up the steps, calling to his brother with no luck stopping him.

"Where are you?" Brad called. "I know you guys are up here." Into each room he looked.

The second floor was much darker than the main floor. In already dark halls Brad looked like a shadow bouncing from room to room. As he rushed by Alex a cool breeze followed suit. Further down the hall it seemed darker, blacker, than the rest of it. Squinting, Alex could just make out two figures in the mass.

Pausing for a moment, Brad noticed his brother's curiosity and followed his gaze. "There you are." He started off towards the figures, but they didn't move. "I know you didn't want him to come along. I know you didn't think I'd notice you two messing around, planning shit behind my back."

"Brad."

"No! Alex, I didn't plan this one, okay. This was all them!" His eyes were glued to the two figures. "We weren't even gonna come here until I told them you were coming with us."

"Brad," Alex said, not too sure how to explain what he was looking at. "Brad, I don't think that's them."

Brad stopped, turning to look at him. "What do you mean that's not them? It's them. They're pranking us, trying to scare you. That's all they wanted to do."

"I really don't think that's them, Brad," Alex kept insisting.

"Yes, it is." He turned back to the two. "Admit it, you two were behind this."

The two figures didn't budge.

"Brad."

Another crash erupted from one of the rooms followed by a thud as Mike and Max fell to the floor.

"I told you not to lean so far," Max grumbled, shoving Mike off of him.

Brad stood there staring at them, frozen in shock and an unnerving confusion. At a loss for words, he watched as his friends helped each other up. Slowly he turned, his body trembling as anger dissipated and fear set in. The figures still stood engulfed in the darkness at the end of the hall.

"What's wrong with him?" Max asked, brushing dust off his shirt. He whacked Mike in the arm. "What's their problem?"

"You don't see them?" Alex asked, fighting off the shakiness of his voice.

"See who?" Mike asked, confused.

"Guess we got 'em good. They're both shaking." Max laughed and proudly elbowed Mike.

"You really don't see them?" Alex asked, redirecting his gaze to the duo.

The two looked at each other then back at Alex, shaking their heads in response.

Gulping, Alex turned back to his brother. "Brad?"

He didn't know what to say. Who or whatever he was looking at was still staring him down.

"Brad?" Alex's voice was nearly a croak.

"When I say run, run," Brad said, eyes still on the figures.

"What are you talking about?" Max asked. "Kid, what's going on?"

"I think they're trying to scare *us* now," Mike joked.

"Heh, that's not gonna happen. Come on, guys, we get it. We got you and you're not happy about it," Max said.

The darkness surrounding the two figures swirled and morphed into a human-like form behind them. Brad and Alex watched in horror, frozen in fear. Brad stumbled back.

"Very funny. Who's that?" Mike asked. "You seeing this, Max?

Max nervously laughed, seeing the taller figure that had formed. "Yeah, I see that. You two really are trying to out scare us."

Brad looked back at them. "Wait, so you can see that one but not the others?" He spun back to the figures and slowly started backing towards his brother. "Alex, when I say run…"

The third figure raised its arms as the two smaller ones giggled in childish glee. It seemed to be holding something.

"Guys?" Max grabbed Mike by the arm, ready to tug him away from whatever was going on.

A soft click filled the air as the two smaller figures stepped aside.

"Run!" Brad yelled, reaching back and grabbing his brother.

A loud crack roared as the four boys bolted it for the stairs, ducking as they ran. In terrified unison they all practically slid down the steps, nearly tripping over one another. At the base of the stairs another figure appeared. The boys screamed, falling back on the steps.

A ghostly voice called out from the figure as it stepped aside, gesturing to the front door as it flung open, "Go, while you still can!"

At the top of the stairs the other figure stood, arm raised and the form of a gun in its ghastly hand.

"Not again!" the other figure yelled, its voice echoing in the ether.

Rushing to the door, the four legged it to freedom as another shot rang out. As they crossed the threshold the door slammed shut behind them. Despite the door being shut, they didn't stop until they reached the sidewalk. Brad reached for his brother, pulling him in for a tight hug. Alex didn't fight it, he let the hug go on as long it needed to be. Mike and Max caught their breath, Mike with his hands on his knees and Max using Mike as an arm rest.

"What just happened?" Mike asked between breaths.

Brad let his brother go and looked back at the house. Alex stood close to him, "I think Robert just saved us."

Relieved to be free, the group wasted no time and started off down the sidewalk back to town. In the cool night breeze, a faint cry could be heard as one more shot rang out. The boys picked up their pace and put as much distance as they could between them and the manor. With the house behind them, it stood silent in the dark of the growing night. In the windows the faint shapes of the figures they'd seen moments before watched the group. One more stood on the front steps before fading into the night. At least one spirit could rest easy knowing they saved another group from meeting the same fate his family did.

The Dark Pine Demon

The large pine towered over the crumbling wall that wrapped around its trunk. Its dark green needles seemed black in the moonlight. It may have sat at the center of town, but between the overgrowth and how far it was from the main roads, it nearly blended into its surroundings. Through the remaining ruins of the wall meant to cut it off from the world, beneath the lower branches, it was like looking into an abyss.

The wall was said to protect the tree, the first true landmark of Dark Pine as it was. It's been debated, though, that it was actually built to protect the world around it. Within that darkness beneath the tree something lurks. It's been there before the town existed. The tree is its home. The wall keeps it in. Simple enough, right?

One of Dark Pine's founders would disagree, and so would every member of their family for generations to come. When Dark Pine planned to make its move, the leader of the group, Stephen Murphy, took a group of men out into the woods to scout for new ground. They stumbled upon a clearing not too far from home. At its center stood the tall pine tree that now looms over the town as a reminder of where it began. What he didn't expect to see, though, was a figure sitting under it.

In the darkness of the shade beneath the needles it sat unbothered by its new visitors. Thinking it was a fellow villager, the Murphy called out.

No answer, just a brief look in their direction before turning its attention back to the distant tree line. After a quick pause he stepped closer, motioning to the others to stay back. The longer he stared into the shadows the figure became clearer. It sat on the ground, its back against the tree's trunk. He couldn't quite place it, but something didn't sit right.

While it seemed human in form, something about it was off, almost uncanny. Normally he'd assume it was just a trick of the light, but even in shadow the figure's skin seemed to have a green hue. Upon closer inspection its legs bent and twisted in an unusual way, almost animal like in nature. Its arms seemed stretched out, its fingers like branches with claw-like talons at their tips.

Murphy tried once more to call out to the figure. Announcing his intentions to survey the land, his voice shook with each word. This time the figure, the creature, reacted. Rolling onto all fours it pushed itself up onto its feet. Hunched over, its arms hung down causing its fingers to drag along the ground beneath it.

Stumbling back, Murphy tripped over his own feet as the creature crawled out from under the tree. As it cleared the bottom layer of needles it rose, standing a good eight feet tall. The rest of the group looked on in horror as it walked over to their leader. Some of them drew their guns, ready to shoot, while the others ran up to Murphy ready to pull him back. The creature bent down to look the leader in the eyes and cocked its head in curiosity.

A slit that seemingly ran through the cracks in the creature's face opened where a mouth would be. A low grunt followed by a breathy rasp of a voice spoke out, "Why have you come here?"

Fear shook the group. Despite how much his knees rattled Murphy stood his ground. "We're here…We're here to survey the land."

The creature tilted its head again in the other direction. "Survey?"

Swallowing a breath, he spoke up. "Our town, we would like to expand it. And this area is the perfect size."

Rising up to its full height, the creature looked down on the group, its gaze shifting from person to person. "For just you few?"

"No," Murphy said. "We were sent here to look at this land."

The creature stood there, examining the men once more. "You mean *my* land," it insisted. In a swift movement the creature bent down and was face to face with Murphy. Where eyes should be, two dim orange dots glowed back. "You thought you could take my home from me?"

Whatever confidence Murphy and his men had vanished completely.

"Do you know what this land is?" The creature asked.

The group remained silent, frozen as the creature towered over them, the large dark pine behind it.

"I thought not." The creature turned to face the tree, looking up at it with respect. "This tree, this land, is more than just my home. It's the center of these woods and the source of its energy. That tree is my home. I live within it. It is a part of me."

After a moment of pause two of the men dropped their guns and ran back to the tree line. The others stayed, waiting for orders. Murphy, though, was still frozen. He knew how this could go and he could see where it was going.

The crack of a line that was the creature's mouth curved downward. "Nothing? Not even an offer? I'm giving you a chance to work this out."

"Sir?" One of the men spoke up, snapping their leader out of the trance the underlying dread had on him.

Clutching his hands into tight fists, letting his nails dig into his palms, he looked up to the creature. "My offer is this."

The creature cocked its head.

"I don't want to fight you, although I fear there's no way to make things right, so I offer you this. We move our town to this clearing and expand and grow calling this our new home. This tree, your home, remains untouched, and you remain unharmed and left to your own devices."

"Hmph." Amused, the creature lowered its hand. "And if you and your men, or anyone in your town disrespect myself or my home? Am I expected to let that go with no consequences?"

"I will take care of it," Murphy insisted.

"I'm sure you will." The creature said. Leaning back down into a menacing hunch, it put a long hand on his shoulder digging its claws in. "But remember," it started. "If anything happens to my home, I *will* return. I will check to see if the problem's been dealt with, and if it hasn't, we will see how well those weapons of yours protect you."

The remaining men raised their guns with shaky hands, unsure of what was going to happen. Murphy stood there, unable to move with the creature's claws still deep in his shoulder.

The creature looked at the remaining men and smiled then returned their gaze to their leader. "Let this mark be a reminder." Blood trickled down from the wounds as it released its grip. "I will be back to check on this land. No warning. No time for preparation. I will return. If I see anything has been destroyed or my tree has been damaged, I will not be as merciful."

As the blood ran down his arm, Murphy watched as the creature turned back to the large pine from which it had sat under only moments prior. Crouching back beneath the bottom layer of needles, it disappeared into the tree's trunk as if by magic. No hole opened up. No door of any sort opened. It just walked into the tree as if it were a part of it.

The group watched in shock, in confusion, but mostly in fear hoping it wouldn't change its mind and come back for them. After a moment of pause the men dropped their weapons and rushed to their leader. One ran to the tree to investigate to no avail. There was no sign the creature had even been there at all.

Despite the concern his men had for him, Murphy didn't move. Whether it was out of fear or to process everything that had happened, he couldn't move. Even as the blood continued to run down his arm from the four gashes left behind, it was as if he were stuck. One of his men shouted to another to run back to town and get help. They tried to comfort him as they waited, but their words fell on deaf ears.

His arm pounded, a mixture of throbbing pain and a burning sensation from the inside out. Each thudding beat of his heart was the only thing he heard as his mind lingered on what ifs. Whatever that thing was, he knew it wasn't gone. Somewhere within that pine it slumbered, waiting. It wasn't necessarily its blessing that he had, more of a word of caution, a warning. What if it was toying with them? What if it only said that to get rid of them? But what if it actually meant it when it said it would only come out if anything happened to the land or the tree? They could still move and build without any interruption if they were careful.

"Sir?"

He continued to stare at the towering pine.

"Sir?"

Murphy cleared his throat. "We'll start building tomorrow."

The remaining men looked at him confused. "But sir, the creature."

Raising a hand to silence them, he turned to face them. "We'll begin building, but no one is to touch or go near that tree." He looked over his shoulder at it. "If that thing means what it said, then we'll build around it."

"And the rest of the land?" another of his men asked.

"The rest of the clearing will become our home. If we have to, we'll build a wall around the tree to keep anyone else from harm," Murphy said. He grasped at his shoulder, wincing. "No one else needs to know."

To his credit, no one knew. No one asked. It wasn't until his family caught him leaving at odd times in the middle of the night that anyone learned the truth. As the town grew the nightly visits became more frequent. One night his son woke to the sound of the front door slamming shut. Sneaking downstairs, he poked his head out the door, finding his father creeping off into the dark of the night. Following not too far behind, he tailed his father all the way to the towering pine. Hidden from view behind a nearby bush, he watched as his father leaned into the wall that surrounded the tree.

It looked like he was inspecting it, checking every crack and crevice, patting it down.

Occasionally he'd pause. In those moments his son could've sworn his father was talking, whether it was to himself or to the wall itself, he never knew, but it was an odd sight for sure. He'd never seen him do a thing like that. His father kept to himself, yes, but was quiet and sure of himself. Here, though, he seemed paranoid, maybe even somewhat hysterical with how he circled and checked the wall. It wasn't until a long spidery hand reached over the wall, he realized.

~

PRESENT DAY

"So why do you have to go then?" Jack asked, swinging his legs off of the edge of his sister's bed as she packed her backpack.

"Because. I'm the oldest and dad's too sick to do the trip," Jess replied, grabbing a flashlight from her desk drawer before sliding it shut.

"Yeah, but there's nothing there to look at. Why do we have to keep this up anyway? Our great great great grandpa or whatever was probably crazy," Jack said.

Shoving a few extra blankets and a jacket into her bag, she turned around, waving her hands as she spoke. "Yeah, I know that, but I promised dad I would. Besides, if there's really nothing there, I shouldn't take too long and I should be back before the movie marathon at nine."

"You sure I can't come with you? I can help," Jack insisted.

"No way. If anything happened to you mom and dad would kill me. You're staying here." She zipped up the last compartment and slung the backpack over her shoulder. "Alrighty, let's do this." Jess took a deep breath and marched out into the hall, her brother right behind her.

Quickly dipping into his room, Jack grabbed his jacket and sprinted down the stairs, rejoining his sister.

As she opened the door she noticed her brother's eager face in the reflection of the frosted glass window on the door. "Jack, what did I say?" Jess spun around to face her little brother, crossing her arms and raising a concerned and frustrated brow.

"Come on. You said it yourself you're only doing this because dad's sick. Next time *he'll* go back to doing the monthly trip." Jack grabbed his sister's arm and stared up at her with wide eyes and a pleading pout.

"Didn't you think this was stupid?" she asked.

"Yeah, but come ooooon," he begged. "How often do we get to do the trip? I already did my homework. Pleeeaaaassssee?"

Jess looked down at her brother. She shrugged and gave a sigh of defeat. "Fine, but stay close. I don't need you to getting lost."

"Yes!" Jack cheered, punching the air in victory.

The two headed out into the darkening night. The deep navy blue of the sky slowly fading to a deep black. They didn't live too far from the center of town, but the walk felt longer when the world was in shadow. Everything looked different somehow.

No one in town really went out past eight or nine in Dark Pine. Too many tales. Too many missing without rhyme or reason throughout the years. While there was a curfew at one point, it was lifted years ago when Jess about nine or ten. It had become second nature to stay in. Unless you worked in one of the shops on Main Street or an office in the small shopping district by the road connecting Dark Pine to its sister town Ceder Creek, most were home already.

Pebbles shot off of the sidewalk as Jack shuffled his feet, kicking up the small patches of dirt at the sides of the path. "What do you think is really behind the wall?"

"Is that why you wanted to come?" Jess asked. "To see what was back there?"

"I mean, our great great great great great great..."

"Jack," Jess grumbled.

"What? He may have been crazy, but what if he was hiding something back there instead and the whole Dark Pine Demon thing was just a way to keep people from finding whatever it was?"

She looked over at her brother, bemused. "Seriously?"

"What?"

"What do you mean what? You basically just said our great great great grandpa was a Scooby Doo villain," Jess joked.

"So, what if he was? You like to write, who's to say it isn't a family *thing*?" Jack suggested.

"A family *thing*?"

"Yeah. What if he was just a *really* good storyteller?"

"A storyteller, right." Jess couldn't believe what she was hearing.

"Is that why you thought it was pointless to keep this up? It's just a story?"

"Yeah. AND the wall is destroyed. It's just rocks in a circle now," Jack said. "What's the point in checking out something that isn't there?"

"I guess you're right," Jess agreed. "There isn't much there anymore. Dad sounded really serious about this though."

"Did he say anything about it?"

"Not much," she started. "Just go to the tree, check the wall, and get out of there… He did say to keep it quick though, and not to talk to anyone or anything. That was a weird rule, now that I'm thinking about it."

"Who did he think would be there?" Jack looked up at his sister.

"No clue. I'm a responsible adult though, I can handle this."

"You're nineteen, how much of an adult are you really?" Jack joked.

"Hey!" she responded, lightly whacking him in the arm. "Well, I wasn't expecting to be babysitting my kid brother while doing this."

"Who are you calling kid? I'm fourteen. I don't need a babysitter. I can take care of myself," he shot back.

Jess put an arm around Jack's shoulders and pulled him in as they continued on their trek. They smiled and laughed. The night didn't feel as ominous as they stuck together, and the road became more overgrown. Turning off into a small dirt path, they held hands to avoid being separated by the brush. No amount of brush and branches though could block the towering shadow of a pine tree in the near distance.

As they got closer the tree seemed to grow. While it was more than likely a trick of the light, its dark green needles blended into a void. The moonlight trickled through the surrounding trees. The two pulled each other closer as they neared the small clearing around the wall.

While the dead patch of grass that sat between them and the wall around the tree, it acted like a moat. They were almost afraid to cross over it. They couldn't quite place it, but a deep feeling of unease set in as if something hidden in the darkness watched them.

"Let's just get this over with," Jess said with a nervous gulp. She gripped her brother's hand tighter, and he gripped hers back in an act of comfort. With a deep breath she led him to the rubble of a wall that surrounded the great old pine.

Stone laid crumbled and chipped at the base of the wall, or what was left. Beyond it the void of the great pine extended beneath it. They slowly circled the perimeter. Some parts of the wall still stood tall with holes like windows looking into the darkness. The lowest points came up about waist high. It may have seen better days, but it was still doing its job, even if it wasn't doing it well. It wouldn't be surprising if people had hopped over to turn it into a hangout. Just beyond a small crack in the wall Jess could see an old spray can with three slashes through its side.

As she looked into the cracks and holes they passed by, Jess squinted trying to see anything. Nothing but black. The wind picked up, whistling in the cool Fall night. The trees around them rustled and swayed, dancing to the tune. Jack grabbed his sister's arm to get as close as possible to her.

Even as the breeze picked up, they continued to slowly circle the wall. Not quite sure what to look for, Jess paused and looked into a nearby hole in the wall.

"What are you doing?" Jack whispered.

"Shhh," Jess hissed, turning to her brother with a finger to her mouth. "Dad said no talking to anyone, remember?"

"Well, you're talking to me," he whispered back, still holding onto her. "Besides, he didn't mean me, remember? Why would he?"

Giving a quick glare she huffed and sighed then returned her gaze to the hole in the wall. "Well, I don't know what he wanted me to look for. He just told me to come here since he couldn't and look at the wall and go."

"Well," Jack started. "We've done that. Now can we go home now, it's getting colder out here."

Squinting a little more she saw a glimmer of light, faint, but visible, nonetheless. "Hold on," she said. "Get my flashlight from the backpack. It's the top zip."

"Why can't you do it?"

"I see something and I don't wanna lose it," she answered.

Begrudgingly, Jack let go of her arm and unzipped the bag. It didn't take much digging to find the flashlight. He zipped the backpack back up and handed the light to his sister. "What do you think it is?"

"I'm not sure, but there's something there," she said, taking the flashlight and pointing it through the hole. With a click of the button a beam of light flooded the space behind the wall. For a brief moment she could see the trunk of the tree and where the bottom layer of needles ended. Beneath it, though, something caught her eye. "Is that an animal?" As she leaned in for a better look the flashlight flickered. "Shit." She stepped back and started whacking the side of the flashlight. "Come on."

"What happened?" Jack asked, his eyes darting between his sister and the hole in the wall. "What'd you see?"

"I don't know," Jess answered, still trying to shake and hit the flashlight in hopes it was just being finicky. "I think it was an animal."

From behind the wall a loud scratching and rustle filled the air.

Jack ran behind his Jess. "What was that?"

"It's just an animal. That's all it is," she said.

The noises got louder, more aggressive.

"We...we should get going. Come on, Jack." Taking her brother's hand, she started backing away, keeping one eye on the hole in the wall.

"Who's there?" a gravelly voice asked from the darkness.

The siblings froze.

The voice spoke up once more, just as gravelly but somehow smoother than before. "Who are you?"

"Jess?" Jack whispered to his sister, hanging onto her arm, hoping for some sort of direction.

The wind picked back up and the voice spoke again. "Are you the new keeper? Where is Miles?"

A sharp chill ran down her spine as she heard the name. "Th…that…that's my dad," she said. *Shit.* Her father's voice echoed in the back of her mind. *I shouldn't have said anything.*

"It's alright," the voice reassured. "I won't tell."

"Jess?" Jack clung to her back, his grip tightening.

"When I say run, you run, alright?" Jess instructed her brother.

"Why, what is it?" Jack peaked over her shoulder but couldn't see anything. "Who is it?"

Through the hole in the wall, within the darkness, a pair of fiery dots of light came closer as the voice called out once more. "A Murphy." The dots, like orangey-red fireflies, tilted, one lower than the other as if looking passed Jess. "And who are you, little one?"

"Don't say anything. Just run when I tell you to and get mom, okay?" Jess commanded.

He could see the dots like glowing eyes through the hole in the wall, looking at him, burning into him. Something in him screamed to run but his body was paralyzed.

"Jack!" Jess snapped at him.

"Right. Yeah." He shook off the fear as best as he could.

"Run straight home, don't look back. Don't stop running until you're back at the house," Jess directed.

The dots returned to Jess. "Home? Hmph. It's been some time since I've seen what's become of mine." The voice almost mocked her with a sandy grit to its already gravelly tone. The dots moved closer, a faint semblance of a face now at the hole, its eyes glowing brighter. A long slit where a mouth should be opened as it spoke again. "Can I tell you a secret?"

Jess stood her ground, one foot angled back ready to run when she could.

"Do you want to know who I am?" the voice asked.

She knew she already broke the most important rule her father wanted her to follow, but something in her insisted she try again. *Just keep your mouth shut. It's easy enough. I just need to get the two of us back in one piece. After that I don't have to worry about doing this again.*

The face bobbed as the slit curved upward into a weird smile and the lights of its eyes dimmed. "Some things never change. You Murphys always find new ways to amuse me." A bassy hum emanated from it. "He didn't tell you, did he?"

Jess took a step back, ready to go. Jack stood behind her, waiting for the signal.

The face dipped back into the darkness, hidden in the void once again. "This little tradition he has you keeping up, it's not to keep me in." A dark hand with long spidery fingers slid over the top of the wall, its skin like bark, as another hand slid in beside it.

Stumbling backwards out of panic, Jess yelled back to her brother, "Run!"

Without hesitation or second thought, Jack ran off into the night in the direction they'd come from. Any thoughts he had of turning back for his sister were overthrown by fear.

Jess continued to stumble and step backwards as a figure rose from behind the wall. Backlit by whatever moonlight seeped through the now overcast sky, its silhouette hung over her like the towering pine it shared a home with. In the dim light it almost looked like another tree, but those glowing eyes burned with an anger that struck a sharp paralyzing fear throughout her body that she'd never felt before.

The figure, the creature, leaned in now almost face to face with her. "Your family has visited for centuries now. Not one of them keeping their promise." It placed a hand on her shoulder, it's branch like talons firmly wrapped around her arm. Pulling her in to bring her even closer, its voice deepened to a gritty bass. "What has become of my home?"

As his feet hit the pavement and his heart beat faster than it'd ever had before, Jack nearly tripped over his feet as a blood curdling scream filled the night air. He didn't need to see it to know what had happened. His gut wrenched and his eyes began to water. He was too close to home to head back to the wall. He could only go home and hope that his parents would know what to do.

The Weeping Widow

Lost in a sea of trees between the old town and the new, within the cemetery of Dark Pine's oldest church, sits a statue. A memorial for a fallen saint. A mother of one of the founding families, Emilia Warran. Dead and fragile vines of ivy and weeds twist and tangle around it, as if trapping her image where it was placed. Emilia was a dedicated wife to Dark Pine's founding father Maxwell Warran and their children Heidy, Hellen, and Joshua. She did what she could to keep them safe and cared for. A fighter to the end, some say.

The game is simple. When the night grows dark you find her grave. Bring a candle of whatever color you choose. Some say to avoid red, the color of love and desire, while others strongly suggest it. Whatever color you choose, one thing is sure, she needs to see your face. Bring an offering to keep her at bay. It should be related to the request you'll make. Many offer her flowers, but anything is fine as long as it makes sense.

"What does that even mean?" Tammy asked, fighting through a handful of hanging branches.

"It means it has to relate to what you ask her for," Derek answered, leading the way through the brush.

"What's next, pricking our fingers and making a deal with the Devil?" Tammy joked.

"Cute. The instructions say to hold the lit candle and recite the incantation," he explained.

"Hmph. Where'd you find this again?"

"I told you," Derek started, trying to fight back embarrassment. "It's just a website."

"*Riiight*…a website," Tammy said. She pushed through another tangle of broken branches to catch up with her boyfriend. "The Dark Pine Depths isn't the most legit source of information, you do realize this, right?"

Derek paused and spun around, shining his flashlight in Tammy's direction. "Look, it's completely legit. You've heard the stories. They're all on there."

Tammy winced, raising a hand to cover her eyes.

"Remember that one about the demon dog at the old warehouse? The one we went to last Summer?"

"Yeah, but that's just a story," Tammy insisted.

"We saw it though," Derek insisted right back.

Sighing and adjusting the strap on her bag, Tammy walked up to him. "What we saw was a stray dog." She put a hand on his shoulder. "It was probably living in the warehouse. It's not that crazy."

"What about earlier this year at the old park? We both saw the figure in the woods. It had to be one of the Silent Watchers," he suggested, the flashlight dancing as he gestured.

"Weren't those at the campgrounds? Besides, it was probably just a tree," Tammy explained.

"Why would one tree stand out more than the others? Why'd it look like a person?"

Tammy shook her head and held onto the strap of her bag that continued to slip off her shoulder. "They're all just stories, and whatever this ritual thing you found on the Dark Pine Depths, it's just a game."

"I know you don't believe in this stuff, but at least humor me?" Derek asked.

"Babe, that's what I've been doing every trip," she reassured him. "Look, I love you and I love seeing you happy and enjoying the things you do. It's fun exploring these places, but sometimes a story is just a story." Sliding the bag off her shoulder and letting it slip to the ground, she put an arm around him. "If anything, at least we know the statue's real. We've seen pictures of it all over town."

Derek looked over to Tammy and gave a weak smile. "Yeah, I guess you're right." He looked down at the paper in his hand. "Can we at least give the ritual a shot anyway?"

"Sure," Tammy said, rubbing Derek's arm to comfort him. "What's this supposed to do anyway?"

"You'll see," he answered, excitedly pulling away from her. "Come on, the statue should be around here somewhere." Redirecting his flashlight, Derek started off in the direction they'd been originally heading.

"That isn't ominous at all," Tammy joked, grabbing her back off of the ground and headed after him.

As the flashlight lit up the path ahead, through the maze of branches a figure stood tall in the distance. Had it not been for the cracks and ivy that wrapped it like a blanket or a natural chain keeping her in place, they would've mistaken it for a person. The statue towered over the shrubs around it. Its head angled downward, looking down at the grave marker it cradled. A long, carved cloak draped over it, trailing to the ground behind the marker, pooling at its sides, almost blending into the overgrowth and grass around it.

Each step closer it became more obvious how she got her name. Upon closer inspection, the years of rain and exposure to the elements created dark, tear-like trails down each eye of the statue that ran down to the stone beneath it. Despite the supposed tears, her expression was somber. A polite and caring smile, one of a mother, carefully carved and preserved in stone for centuries to come. If it weren't for her surroundings, she'd seem welcoming to approach.

To her sides, hidden beneath the other brush were the cracked and broken remains of other gravestones from the old cemetery. The old church wasn't too far away, a shadow in the background, just as swallowed by the forest around it as everything else as a tree twisted and reached out of the old bell tower.

They dropped their bags at the base of the grave. In the light of the flashlight the tears of the statue seemed to disappear as Derek panned over it.

"There she is," he said.

Tammy didn't know what to say. Like a moth drawn to the flame, all she could do was move closer.

"She's beautiful, right?" Derek asked, just as fixed on the statue as his girlfriend was.

She didn't know what to say. Instead, she just stepped back and examined the statue and grave as a whole.

"So…you wanna give the game a shot now?" Derek asked, waving a hand in front of her face.

Snaping out of whatever hold the statue had on her, she swatted his hand away. "Sure, yeah. Let's get this over with." She looked back up at the statue as Derek emptied his backpack. "Let's make it quick. I don't what it is about this thing, but I think we shouldn't stay too long."

Amused, Derek paused for a moment as he set up the items. "Afraid she'll come to life or something?"

"What?! No way." Tammy walked over to where he was setting up an old dish towel like a mat and laying out different items. "It's just getting dark out, and we don't know what's out here. There could be wolves or something." She looked around, out into the woods around them that were getting darker with each minute they spent there. "I heard some reports of bears in the area."

"We're fine. If we need to we can stay in the old church," he assured her as he fought with a white tapered candle that wouldn't stand in the holder he bought from the local dollar shop.

Hunching over to get a better look at what Derek had placed on the towel, Tammy spotted some familiar faces. In front of the candle holder was a photo of them from their first date at the Fall festival last year. They had a small photo booth and he insisted they hop in and take a few photos. "Why is this here?"

"Oh, that…uh…" Derek panicked. "Can you hold the instructions for me?" Shoving the packet of paper into Tammy's hands, he returned to rummaging through the bags.

A little put off, she continued to watch him place various things out on the towel. The printed packet hung in her hands, a creased mess of text and smudged images. She looked down at it for a second. The words "The Widow's Wish" followed by an overly edited photo of the statue caught her eye. "What is this?"

"It's a game if that makes you feel better," Derek said.

"A game. This is supposed to be a game?" She flipped through the pages. Between paragraphs were lists of items and instructions. A section marked "Rules" and "Warnings" stuck out. "And you said this was from the Dark Pine Depths, right?"

"Yup," he said, unphased by the question and still setting up his alter of items at the base of the gravestone. "Just have one more thing to do and we'll be good to go." He pulled out a long candle lighter. With a flick of the switch a small flame popped up, emitting a faint orange light.

"You've got to be kidding."

"Nope." Lowering the lighter to the tip of the tapered candle, he lit the wick and flicked off the lighter. "Alright, hand me the instructions. Let's get this started."

Tammy watched as he knelt in front of the statue, the packet in hand, and began reading from the paper.

"According to this, once the candle is lit, the game begins," he said. His eyes remained glued to the page as Tammy stood back and watched.

In the light of the candle, she could see him squinting at the paper. "Need me to grab the flashlight, babe?"

"No, I've got this," he insisted. "Ahem…Weeping Widow, founding mother, we call on you now to grant us our wish."

"We?"

Turning to her for second, "It's just what the paper says, don't worry," he reassured her. Eyes back on the page and facing the statue once again, he continued on. "We've come to you with an offer. An offer for a wish." Reaching into his coat pocket he pulled out a chain. From the palm of his hand a charm slid, pulling the chain further from his grasp as he gripped it tighter.

Leaning in, Tammy recognized the shape. A love heart with a small key attached to the loop that held it on the chain. She grasped her neck, patting her chest in a frantic realization. It was hers. "When the hell did you take that?" She marched forward, pushing the packet down and out of his face.

"Look, you'll thank me when this is done."

Her brows furrowed and she reached for the chain. "There's no way you're giving anything of mine as any offering."

Raising his arm, he pulled it out of reach. "I can get you another one, I promise."

The two stumbled and fumbled in a dance of frustration. Tripping over Derek's feet, Tammy fell to the ground.

"Shit. I'm sorry. Hold on." Derek pocketed the necklace and reached down to help, only to be met with a swat of the hand.

"Don't bother," Tammy snapped. Helping herself up, she grabbed her bag from the base of the statue.

"What are you doing? We barely even started the ritual," he said in desperation.

"I'm leaving, Derek. I didn't sign up for this." Tammy looked up at the statue, its tear-like cracks and crevices looking darker somehow in the candlelight. "I don't know what you plan on asking for, but I want nothing to do with it."

Reaching out to her, Derek begged, "Come on Tam, I'm doing this for us."

"For us?" she fumed. "Is this a ritual or a game, Derek? Because whatever it is, I wasn't told anything about it. I've gone with you to all of these different places and supported your interest in them. I've stood by you each time, even when you've thought you encountered something from one of the local legends and it turned out to be a stray dog or something." She marched up to him, now as close as possible to him, eyes glaring in anger. "I loved you, Derek. I did. I even enjoyed these trips. They were genuinely fun. But this is where I draw the line. Whether I believe in this stuff or not, I'm not being brought into some sick ritual you didn't even tell me anything about."

At a loss for words, Derek stood frozen.

"Say something," Tammy demanded, fighting back welling tears.

He couldn't. His thoughts raced as he continued to stand there.

"Okay then," she said, nodding a nod of defeat and understanding. "Have fun. I'm heading back to the car. When you're done with whatever this is, you're dropping me off at my place and then we're done." With slow steps she backed away before turning around and pulling out the extra flashlight she'd packed.

It was just him now. Alone with the widow. Alone with his thoughts. His grip tightened on the packet. Despite the first instinct to hold it back, he let the tears break through. One by one they fell before they turned into a seemingly unstoppable stream down his cheeks.

"What is your wish?" a woman's voice asked as the wind picked up.

Sniffling, Derek wiped his face as dry as he could with his jacket sleeve. Looking around he couldn't see anyone. "Tammy, is that you?"

The wind picked up once more, swirling around him making the flame of the candle dance. With it the voice returned in a soothing tone. "What is your wish, my child?"

Blinking and rubbing his eyes, he tried to look around again with no luck. Just him, the statue, and the gravestone it guarded. Defeated and disappointed he let himself sink to the ground. Seated at the base of the grave, the towel laid out before him, the wind picked up stronger than before. The dim light of the candle grew as the flame danced and dipped.

"Let me see your face," the voice requested.

"Wh…what?" Derek choked out, still sniffling.

"Look up."

Raising his head, his eyes followed the light up to the face of the statue now looking down at him. Its tears were more visible than before. In the candlelight the eyes blinked, causing him to shuffle and crawl back.

"Don't be afraid. You called me and now I'm here to grant your wish."

"My wish?" As much as he wanted to believe what he was seeing, it felt like a prank, a sick joke, maybe even a hallucination.

The statue's eyes seemed to move, looking down at the towel and the items spread out on it. "She's the one who left. A nice girl. A sweet girl, yes?"

He looked down at the photo, Tammy's smiling face looking up at him. As upset as he was, he couldn't help but smile back.

"I take it your wish was for her?" the voice asked.

Gulping and clearing his throat, he answered, "Yes. But…" He looked over towards the path back to the car.

"But she left you. Is that correct?"

He nodded.

"What was your offering?"

He reached into his jacket pocket and pulled out the necklace. "She always wore it."

"And you took this from her," the voice said in an accusing tone.

Back at the car Tammy waited, leaning against the driver's side door and looking at her phone. No signal so not much to do. The battery was half full. Not wanting to waste it, her time checks were brief. Darker and darker the night became. Time felt slower. Impatience turned to paranoia with no sign of Derek.

"Maybe I should head back." She stared off down the path they took. A faint distant glow a good distance ahead through the trees was the only sign they'd even been there. While she couldn't see him, she figured it was safe to assume he hadn't left yet. *Why would he leave the candle burning if he wasn't there? He has to be there, and when he gets back we're getting the hell out of here*, she thought. Her eyes remained glued to the glow.

The wind picked up, kicking up the leaves around her. Stronger and stronger it became. Covering her eyes with her arm to avoid the dirt and dust being swept up in the breeze, she decided to try the car door. She didn't remember if he'd locked it, but it was worth a shot if it could get her out of this wind.

Despite how hard she tugged at the handle the door didn't budge. As she gave the handle one more pull, a deafening scream echoed through the air. "Derek!" Whipping around, she bolted it in the direction of the glow. Another scream rang out as the candlelight vanished.

Shoving branches and shrubs out of her way as she ran, she stumbled her way through the path until she tripped over something. Feeling around for anything, her hand landed on the cylindrical tube of the flashlight. She fumbled with it until she found the switch. On the ground before her was the sleeve of Derek's jacket, but no sign of Derek himself. Rushing to her feet she panned the flashlight around.

At the base of the grave his backpack sat mostly untouched, open and full of leaves now from the strong winds. The towel Derek placed out was laying draped over the gravestone, covering the text. As the light moved upwards, a glint of light reflected off of the statue's hands. Hanging from its fingers was her necklace, swinging in the now gentle breeze.

Taking the necklace, Tammy stepped back, clutching it in her hand. "Derek?!" She called out, never more desperately hopeful for a response.

Silence. No response other than the whistle of the wind.

"Derek? Where are you? This isn't funny."

Another breeze picked up in response. Within the whoosh of the wind a voice answered. "Despite the sacrifice you still came back."

Tammy whipped the light in the direction of the voice, falling on the crying face of the statue.

"A stolen offering is not a fair trade," it whispered.

She looked down at the necklace.

"You're not to blame. It was stolen from you," it assured her.

"This isn't real," Tammy denied.

Another breeze swirled around her as the voice answered again. "I'm afraid it is, my dear."

She looked up at the statue, its eyes weirdly meeting hers.

"You've done all you could to take care of him. You've made him happy. But has he done the same for you?"

The breeze swirled again, spinning her around to face a now darkened path with the old church towering over.

"I know your pain. You've supported him with no return, yet here you are," the voice hissed. "I admire your dedication, dear, but he has to answer for his misdeeds."

Tammy looked deep into the darkness ahead.

"Let your light guide you. The church will be your safety, but for him, I'm afraid it won't do much now."

A strong gust forced her forward as thunder rumbled in the distance. A quick flash of light followed as rain began. Flipping up her jacket hood, she started off to the church. The flashlight barely made a difference given the void of the darkness that came with the night. Heavier and heavier the rain came down making it harder to keep her footing. Despite the occasional slips of her sneakers on the wet leaves, she kept going.

Luckily the church wasn't as far from the grave as she'd thought. The flashlight may not have been much help, but it did the job. In the dark of the night the white siding of the old church almost glowed in the light. Through a broken door barely hanging on by its hinges, a row or two of pews could be seen. Hope set in as she ran for the entrance.

"Derek, just stay right there! I'm coming to get you!" Tammy called out.

Upon entering the building, the rainfall sounded more like hail against the roof. Shining the flashlight around the room, she spotted an old confessional booth in the far corner. In one of the doors a figure stood, but she couldn't make it out.

"Derek?" Without hesitation, she hurried over. "Just stay there, we can wait out the storm here." As Tammy got closer, the figure entered the booth. She followed after. Arriving at the door, she shined the flashlight into the booth. "Derek?"

It was empty. She pushed on the divider with her free hand to make sure it didn't open, no luck.

Dipping her head into the other side of the booth, it was just as empty. Returning her focus to the side she was on, she cautiously stepped in. Not a single handle or panel to push back. No way he could've escaped.

"Derek, come on? You don't even wanna know what I had to go through to get here." Examining the booth further, the light landed on the seat. A familiar face. A photo strip. The photo from the carnival. Flipping it over as she picked it up, she noticed something on the back. A phrase. "You stole her heart and offered it on a chain. The widow will not help you, you must feel her pain."

The Silent Watchers

Within the forest, the remains of the old border stood. Now a crumbling wall of stone, it served as a reminder of where Dark Pine got its start. While the old town had been reclaimed by the forest that surrounded it, the border still served as a window to the past. Through the trees, if you look hard enough, you can see through to the old clearing. The edges of old homes were just barely in view. But sometimes, sometimes it was more than a window.

The Dark Pine campgrounds weren't too far from the border. As far as the camp was concerned the border kept people from venturing too far out into the woods. Every week was a new tale from visitors to the grounds, and every story eerily similar. They heard voices and rustling from within the woods, and when they went to check it out, just beyond the wall was someone standing there watching. The voices would stop once they'd been spotted, then an uncomfortable silence that grew until it felt as if the whole forest was a quiet void. Not a single bird or bat, not even the rustle of leaves in the late-night breeze. Just silence. Nothing else.

While for most locals it was a nice weekend getaway, it was also a place for the curious. The old border drew a crowd. This night was no different for the Haunters, a small paranormal team from a few towns over. They apparently gained quite the following.

"Are you sure you don't want anyone to stick around?" Tilly asked, one elbow resting on the base of the open car window. "We can't just leave y'all alone up here."

"Look, it's part of the deal. We go to a place, we're usually locked in, and we investigate. The only people asking questions are usually us," Chad explained. "It's how we've always worked."

Tilly smirked. Looking into the van, she eyed the other haunters. "Well, this isn't like the other places you've been. I can't lock you in, and I can't leave you alone."

Chad shuffled in his seat, fumbling through his jean pockets. "What if we made a deal?" he asked, pulling out his wallet.

"Woah there, buddy," Tilly said, raising a hand to stop him. "I'm not riskin' my job for a bribe."

"It's not a bribe," Chad insisted, taking out a small handful of cash. "Consider it extra pay."

Tilly raised a brow unimpressed.

Chad flipped through his wallet a little more and pulled out a few extra dollars to add to the handful. Before he could speak, Tilly shifted her stance and stood tall.

"You can keep it. I'm stayin' with you four whether you like it or not." Hands on her hips, she shifted her stance. "For this one, fellas, consider me a part of the team."

The crew exchanged glances, a few groans and unhappy faces.

"Sorry to burst your bubble," Tilly said. "This is my territory, boys. No one's gone beyond that wall, and if anything happens to you, that's on me."

"Fine," Chad grumbled, putting the cash back in his wallet. He looked out the window at Tilly, making sure their eyes met. "But we run the show here for the night. Alright?" "

"Alright," she agreed. "But if anything, and I mean anything starts to go wrong, I'm intervening."

With a sigh of defeat, Chad slumped in his seat. "Okay." He looked into the rearview mirror and back to Tilly. "You can help Ethan, he films everything."

Ethan, one of the two in the backseat, raised a hand giving a shy wave in response.

With a shrug and a nod, Tilly agreed. "Just tell me when you're ready to get started, and I'll make sure you haven't left for the wall without me." She waved them on to the campsite they'd be staying at.

The site wasn't too big. Big enough for a small family to set up camp, but small enough for a couple or single camper to feel comfortable. The Haunters' van took up about half of the space. A few hours had passed as they'd set up some tables and tents. By the time Tilly stopped by the crew was gearing up to head out.

"Heading out without me?" Tilly joked, walking up to the tables they'd propped up. She picked up a gadget from the table closest to her. It had a strip of different colored lights and a needle on it.

"Careful with that," Chad snapped, snatching the gadget away.

Tilly watched as the other two grabbed cameras and a few weirder looking gadgets. She'd seen similar things from other campers over the years, usually teens thinking it was a fun ghost story. These were all labeled and organized, some packed in their own custom cases.

While Chad placed the gadget back, he waved for her to follow him. Leading her to the biggest tent, he showed her a stack of three monitors. "Welcome to homebase. We've already setup some cameras around the site." He pointed to each one. "This one is just outside the camp, covering the campsite itself in case anything happens here. This one's aimed at the wall itself to give us a good view beyond it." He tapped the screen of the third screen. "And this one, this is a feed of our cameras. Each one is from the handhelds. The top left is mine, the top right is Ethan's, and the bottom left is Liam's. This last one on the bottom right is to the left of the wall aiming down it in case anything crosses over the wall."

She had to admit, she was impressed. They may have seemed like another group of kids coming around here "ghost hunting" for fun, but these three had it all worked out. Their cameras were even more professional grade compared to the usual phone videos she'd gotten used to seeing. "You really think you're gonna catch something?" Tilly asked, sounding more curious than condescending.

"You bet," Chad said. He reached down to his hi and grabbed a walkie talkie that was clipped to his belt. Pressing a button, the walkie beeped to life. "You all ready? Ethan?"

The walkie crackled. "Ready," Ethan answered.

"Liam, you good to go?" Chad asked.

The walkie crackled again. "All good here," Liam confirmed.

Chad picked up a walkie from the table and handed it to Tilly. "If you're going to help us, you'll need one of these." He pointed to the entrance of the tent. "Stand over there and I'll test your walkie."

"What?" Tilly responded, sounding a little insulted.

"If I use this too close to your walkie it's gonna be all loud ear-piercing interference. Just trust me on that," he explained.

"Okay," she said, moseying over to the entrance. To be honest, she didn't use her own walkie much with the other rangers in the area. She spent more of her time in the main cabin at the camp entrance. If she ever contacted anyone else it was either by phone or radio. The walkies never really got much use.

Chad pressed down on his walkie. "Tilly?"

Her walkie chirped to life, Chad's voice calling to her. She held it up to her mouth and pressed the button, answering back, "Loud and clear."

"Alright," Chad started. "Looks like we're good to go." He pressed the button on his walkie one more time. "Let's meet up outside homebase and get ready to record the intro." He eyed Tilly, gesturing to leave the tent.

She gave him a glare and he raised his hands as if to say "sorry, my bad" before walking by her to exit the tent. The four met up in the middle of the campsite, the three guys with their cameras in hand and Tilly standing arms crossed. As the three guys discussed the plans for the video intro, Tilly watched torn on whether to be impressed or insulted as she listened to Chad explain the setup.

"We've already shot the story behind the wall and the border of the old town. We've talked about the experiences people have had," Chad said. "Let's grab the EMF readers and flashlights. Ethan, you and…"

"Tilly. You can call me Tilly," she said.

"You and Tilly will follow me and Liam while I show the audience around the site and to the wall," Chad suggested.

Liam raised a hand, almost hitting his cap brim in the process. "We should have her watch the monitors. It could save us some time."

The three looked at Tilly who stood there, an overwhelming sense of nerves taking over. She'd taken on rowdy campers, scared off the occasional bear, even had to wrestle a drunk or two to the ground. For some reason, and she couldn't quite

90

place why, but being stuck in the middle of the three of them unearthed a fight or flight response.

Before she could say anything, Chad nodded. "Tilly, you can stay back here and man the cameras. You said you wanted to keep an eye on things anyway, this'll give you the best chance to watch us all at once."

"All at once?" Tilly didn't like the sound of that. "What exactly does that mean?"

"You'll see," Chad said before turning his attention to Ethan. "Get the camera ready, let's start this thing."

Ethan raised the camera and gave Chad a countdown.

Without time to process anything, Tilly was being introduced to the camera by Chad. His words sounded like a muffled radio as Tilly tried to catch up. It all happened so fast. Before she knew it, she was watching them walk away towards the tree line around the campsite. Chad gestured wildly as he spoke. He made the wall sound like a portal to Hell, the border between worlds or something.

She walked over to the tent, deciding it was easier to watch them without having to hear them talk about the wall like it was evil. Yeah, it had some graffiti on it, a few random symbols here and there that could maybe be seen as demonic. She's been there every time a crew was sent in to scrub the paint off since it's still visible from the campsite. As she watched them on the monitors she smirked, guessing what they were saying.

She chuckled. "They're probably not even actually talking about the original town or what the wall was put there for." In a mocking tone she joked, "And if you look through this dip in the wall a creature from the depths of Hell may jump out at you."

On the monitors the little screens for Chad and Liam's cameras sparked to life. It took a brief moment to adjust from a blinding white to a green and white picture. It was already getting dark enough for the depths of the woods to become visible on the night vision. Ethan's was already on. He must've changed the settings for the filming earlier. On the wider shot Tilly could see Chad directing the others, pointing in various directions.

"Looks like the haunting's begun," Tilly sarcastically said. Her walkie beeped to life.

"How are things looking at home base?" Chad asked. She could see him propping one of the gadgets he brought with him and a small flashlight on top of the wall.

She grabbed her walkie and responded, "It's all good here." Squinting, she looked at the other monitors. "What am I supposed to be looking for anyway?"

The walkie chirped in response before Chad's voice came through. "You know the stories. Just keep your eyes on the wall and look for anyone around it that isn't us three."

"Got it," Tilly said. She glanced over at the camera looking over the wall. As if on cue, she spotted a shadow in the distance beyond the wall. "Okay, very funny. Which one of you is playing with me?"

"What do you mean?" Chad asked. "You see something?"

"Which one of you is out there?" She asked, her voice becoming more annoyed with each word. "I get you guys didn't want me to keep an eye on things, but…" Her gaze shifted to the third monitor, Ethan and Liam's cameras were both bouncing as they walked back towards Chad. Her heart sank.

"Tilly? Tilly, you there?" Chad asked.

She looked back at the shot over the wall and the shadow was gone.

"I'm sending Ethan back to camp to watch the monitors with you," Chad said with a new determination.

Sure enough, Ethan's camera bounced and bobbed with the campsite in view. He must've been running considering how blurred the image was. Even with him on the way, she returned her gaze to the camera pointed over the wall. Nothing.

Ethan popped his head into the tent, camera pointed towards Tilly. "Everything alright in here? I heard over the walkie, you saw something?"

Her eyes remained glued to the screen, refusing to believe it was actually something and not just one of the guys. "There was a shadow right there." She pointed to the spot on the monitor. "I could've sworn there was someone there."

Ethan leaned in closer, aiming the camera at the screen. "And you're sure it wasn't a tree or an animal?"

She shifted her stance, baffled by the question. "I've worked here for five years now, I know the shadow of a person when I see it," Tilly explained.

"Do you think it could've been one of our shadows? Like maybe the flashlight cast it out there?" he suggested.

"That was too far out for it to be that. I've been watching these screens the whole time. The only one near there was Chad, he was playing with that reader thing you guys have and a flashlight," she said. "He was more off to the side for it to even be his if it were from one of you."

The two watched the screens for a moment, tracking Chad and Liam. They seemed to have met up and began discussing something. In the long shot looking down the side of the wall Liam looked more concerned than anything. Chad, on the other hand, seemed eager to investigate further.

Ethan grabbed his walkie. "How are things back by the wall?"

On the cameras they watched Chad reach for his walkie. "I'm thinking it's time to take this investigation a little further."

Ethan spoke into the walkie again, "Are you sure? I didn't get anything down by the other end of the wall. Liam, what about you, you took the other end of the wall."

Liam picked up his own walkie, "Nope. Not a thing. I did think I heard something, but I thought it was probably a deer or something."

"Was it by the wall?" Ethan asked.

"I think it was," Liam answered, unsure of his own experience. "We're literally in the middle of the woods, it could've been anything."

Through the screens Tilly could see Chad becoming more irritated. Before he could answer, the two watched as Chad and Liam bickered. Light shoves and finger pointing was exchanged. Ethan zoomed in on the screen with his camera.

Tilly judged. "Really?"

"What? It's good content," he explained with a shrug.

Shaking her head, she sighed and watched the other monitors. Her eyes widened as she looked at the view over the wall. "Ethan," she said with a gasp, tapping him in the arm. "It's back."

He whipped the camera over to the other monitor, adjusting the zoom. Sure enough, just beyond the wall a shadowy figure stood. They watched in disbelief as the figure tilted its head, looking towards Chad and Liam. Ethan pressed the button on the walkie again. "Guys?"

Didn't matter what angle they looked at, the two were deep in their debate.

Ethan tried again. "Guys, the wall! We've got company!"

It took them a moment to realize what he'd said. Chad finally picked up his walkie. "What did you just say?"

Liam looked over the wall while Chad waited for a response. He smacked Chad in the arm and pointed in the direction of the figure. On the wide shot of the wall, it looked like a standoff. Chad and Liam vs. the mysterious figure. Further back another figure appeared. The first one looked back, acknowledging its new friend. They each looked back at the boys.

Chad and Liam didn't move. They couldn't. What could you do in a moment like that? Tilly exchanged a brief glance with Ethan and eyed the walkie.

"What do I even say?" Ethan says.

"We should get out there," Tilly said, grabbing her walkie and then Ethan's arm.

"Wait, you want us to go out there? Where those things are?" He asked pulling back.

"Yes. Yes I am," she said. "I'm the ranger here. It's my job to make sure y'all are alright and leave in one piece. Let's go." She tugged on his arm again and led him out of the tent. Pulling him along, she marched through the trees.

By the time they got to Chad and Liam, the figures had come together on the other side of the wall. Seeing them in person vs. on the screen, they went from seeing a vague human-like shape to two very human forms. Even in the dark of the night, the figures stood out as if it were just a little shade. If she hadn't known they weren't supposed to be there, she'd have mistaken them for extra members of the Haunters.

The two figures looked like any other person. From where the four stood they could just make out the details of the outfits. Their clothes looked older, more like something you'd see in a historic area. Between the jackets, the vests, and even the more fitted pants with the riding boots. One of them wore an old soldier's hat. Their expressions were just as confused and a little scared.

After a deafening silence that not even the wildlife interrupted, Chad elbowed Ethan. "Make sure you're getting this," he whispered. Keeping his own camera pointed at the figures, he spoke up. "Hello! My name is Chad! My friends and I are here to spend the night. Who are you?"

"What are you doing?" Tilly asked in a hushed tone, leaning into Chad's side.

He whispered out of the corner of his mouth to answer, "Getting answers. Trust me on this." Taking a step forward, he raised a hand and placed it on the wall. Addressing the figures again, Chad spoke up. "Is it alright if I join you?"

While they didn't expect much, one of the figures stepped forward, its mouth moving with no sound to be heard. It wasn't clear what they were trying to say, but the closest of the figures waved an arm, gesturing to come over. Without thinking, Chad started to climb over the wall, partly sitting on the top of it.

"Dude?! What are you doing? Are you nuts?" Liam reached out for his friend. "They could be playing with us."

Chad pulled his arm away, shrugging Liam off. "Look, do you want answers or not?"

Ethan lowered the camera and stepped forward, joining Liam in his concern. "Yeah, we do, but they could be dangerous."

Tilly pushed through the pair. "As the ranger here, I'm ordering you to stand down and stay here. I don't have a good feeling about this. This isn't worth whatever *truth* you're trying to get from this."

Chad paused for a moment. He looked back and forth from Tilly and his team to the two figures, standing there watching. "We started this series to find stuff like this. They literally appeared out of nowhere." He looked at Tilly. "Does the old town have a historic society of any kind with reenactors or anything like that? Anyone that could be out here this close to the old town?"

Shaking her head, she answered. "Not at the moment. I know there are plans to eventually start something like that up, but the town hasn't agreed on it yet."

Chad seemed more than happy with that answer. "Alright then. Unless it's someone playing a prank on us knowing we're in the area, I'm going to check it out." Before anyone could respond, Chad hopped down the other side of the wall and started walking to the figures, his camera raised.

Liam and Ethan froze, unsure of what to do, but Tilly wasn't about to let anything happen. Adrenaline kicked in and she jumped the wall.

As Chad approached the figures, one of them reached out a welcoming hand. The closer to the figures he got the more it looked like they were placed into the world around them. The woods around him were nearly pitch black at this point, yet they could be seen clear as day. With each step closer the sound of distant voices and activity could be heard. Despite the lack of anyone else for miles aside from the others, it was like someone turned on a radio. Children laughing, horses and chickens making noise, hammering, and more, all suddenly a background track to the moment.

Tilly sprinted after him, slipping on leaves and stumbling over twigs and tree roots. She could see the figures speaking, but nothing came out. Even with their silence, as she approached them the quiet of the forest became full of life. As if a switch was flicked, the silence was broken. The suddenness of it all stopped her dead in her tracks. She could see Chad about to take the figure's hand. "Chad, don't!"

As they clasped hands, the sound faded. The forest returned to its usual quiet self. Along with it, though, Chad and the figures he'd joined vanished. As if they blipped from existence, they were gone.

"Chad?!" Tilly couldn't believe her eyes. "Chad?!" She ran to the spot they were stood and found nothing, just disturbed dirt and leaves.

Liam and Ethan followed after as they realized what happened. Grouping around the spot where Chad stood, they shared looks of shock and confusion.

"What happened?" Ethan asked.

"I don't know," Tilly started. "He was here and then he wasn't and the sound..." She spun around, eyes darting between the distant trees, hoping to find him hiding somewhere.

"Wait, wait, wait. Sound? What sound?" Liam asked, putting a hand on her shoulder.

"It was like it went from nothing, no sound, to alive with animals and people and I...I don't know," she explained, still processing what had happened.

Ethan whipped around and started rushing back to the wall. Tilly and Liam followed after, trying to catch up. They each hopped the wall like it was nothing as they sprinted back to the campsite. Ethan was frantic, almost throwing his camera to dig through the bags for their phones.

Liam tried to comfort his friend and coworker, as Tilly walked over the main tent. If there was anything that could help them figure things out, it's the cameras. She knew what she saw. She knew what she heard. It all happened so quickly. He was here and then he wasn't. That's what she knows. In all of her time in the camp watching over the different sites, she'd never seen anything like this happen. Plenty of people have stayed at that campsite hoping to see what the wall was about, but this was a first.

Ready to rewind the footage, something caught her eye. One of the cameras wasn't like the others. Looking at the split screen of the boys camera feeds, the other two were as expected. Ethan's was on the ground, looking at their feet. Liam's was randomly moving around, he was more than likely talking to Ethan. Chad's though. Night vision was still on, but instead of showing the trees around it, it showed the backs of the two figures as they led the way.

Not wanting to take her eyes off of the screen, fearing it might change if she did, she called out to the others. "You need to see this!"

Ethan and Liam stopped what they were doing. They both rose to their feet in unison and hurried over to the tent.

"What is it?" Liam asked, his eyes landing on the monitors. "Is that Chad's camera?"

Ethan pushed him out of the way and joined Tilly at the table. Sure enough, Chad's camera was still on and filming. Liam cautiously walked over and huddled in with the others.

"Please tell me y'all are seeing this too," Tilly said.

Ethan gave a quick "Uh huh."

"I see it, but I'm not believing it," Liam said.

"And those are the same figures we saw," Ethan said.

The three watched as Chad followed the two into an opening in the trees. At first it looked unfamiliar. Horses walked behind wooden fences. Chickens ran freely in the path. An active community was out and about. Older colonial style homes spanned the area and a giant tower loomed in the distance. Ethan and Lima may have been lost, but Tilly recognized it. It was the old town, but somehow not at the same time. Last she'd heard or seen of the place it was overgrown and abandoned, yet there it was.

The three leaned in closer.

"Can we get any audio?" Tilly asked.

Ethan answered, "We'd need his camera, and I mean…" He gestured towards the screen.

As Chad made his way further into the town the feed flickered as static began to swallow the image. Liam whacked the side of the monitor in desperation. Though it briefly seemed to solve the problem, the feed was overtaken by static before fully cutting. Between the three of them it was a shared feeling of disbelief.

In a moment of desperation, Ethan grabbed his walkie and walked to the entrance of the tent. "Chad, can you hear me? Chad?"

Nothing but a buzz of static in return.

They exchanged looks.

"What do we do now?" Liam asked.

Tilly gulped. She knew this technically fell on her. Taking a deep breath, she stood tall. "Okay." She looked back at the screen and then to the mountain of tech beside the table. "We need to make sure we have everything. This is all saved, right?"

Ethan nodded.

She looked to Liam. "I'm going to need you to help me out here. Do you have any sort of team of higher ups to call?"

"Yeah… I'll have to see if I have their info, if not, I'll check Chad's phone. He doesn't have a passcode on it," Liam said.

"Okay…okay…" Tilly took a few more deep breaths to collect herself. "You two stay here and do what you can to get in contact with your team and preserve any of the footage. I'll head back to the main cabin and radio the emergency response team and any other rangers that may be able to help."

Despite what they did, the hope they had, the shared disbelief, Chad was gone. Maybe not in the most conventional sense or reasonable one. They saw what they saw. They all did. Even if no one else believed them or the footage, it happened. There will always be more like the Haunters, more like Chad, desperate for answers. Curiosity is a persuasive feeling, but you never know where it'll take you.